Deadly Quiet

D0967335

K. Bastet

Lisa —
So nice to meet
you, hope you enjoy
my book

Kathryn Comstock

Published by Venture Ink Publishing, Kenosha, Wisconsin
www.ventureinkpublishing.com

Cover Illustration by K. Comstock

DEDICATION

For those who are compelled to struggle with the written
word and follow the old adage...try and try
again...Godspeed

CONTENTS

ACKNOWLEDGMENTS

To my writer's group, so much of what I accomplish
comes from your encouragement.

To my daughter and son, whose love and support carries
me in all my endeavors.

Deadly Quiet

CHAPTER I

There was that odd rustling noise in the hallway again tonight, but Sally was too tired to get up and look. Perhaps one of the cats finally came home. One cat hadn't come home for two nights in a row, and last night the second cat didn't come home either.

Sleep had been a problem for Sally since her daughter left for college two years ago. Locking the bedroom door and taking a light sleeping pill helped her a bit now. But tonight she was anxious about falling asleep; that's when the dream always came, so she'd been in bed by ten thirty. She always tried waking herself, but it was like searching for the hidden door in a circus fun house, no way out. She'd had the same dream since she was a little girl.

The rustling noise was louder tonight like something very heavy was being dragged down the hallway. Sally thought she'd heard it other nights lately, but was never sure the sound wasn't part of a dream. She'd struggle to wake from her drugged sleep and stagger from bed to check, but there was never anything there. In her restless sleep she'd drift back to when she was seven years old and lived in a small Illinois town. The town was surrounded by farm land and there wasn't much to do. Television had only a few programs and kids were supposed to be outside when their chores were done. Warm summer evenings were spent playing Kick the Can in the small park near Sally's house.

Sally was the only girl and she got dirty enough for the sweat to make clean streaks down her face--when there was a fight she was right in the middle. Sally was the smallest and could be quite ferocious; some of the boys got pretty upset if she bested them in a fight.

The dream sequence occurs on one of those hot, sweaty afternoons after a particularly acrimonious ball game. There's a scuffle and she's in the thick of it, as usual. She tucked her shirt into her jeans and tightly cinched her belt when one of the bigger boys grabbed her by the arms. His friend snatched the back of her shirt at the collar and pulled it open. A third boy dropped a large, angry garter snake down her shirt. The last thing Sally always saw before she woke in a frigid sweat was its cold eyes staring into hers, and its scarlet, forked tongue lashing in and out seconds before it went down her shirt.

The snake thrashed and writhed and bit. Sally screamed and screamed, jumping about trying to pull her shirt from her pants.

"I'll kill you for this, Tommy," she'd gasped between sobs.

"Not so tough now, are you," Tommy jeered.

The boys laughed until tears striped their dirty cheeks; that is, until Sally's older brother came and the boys went running. He'd heard her screams a block away.

"Okay, Sally," her brother said after he'd calmed her down, "You can't tell mother. You know what will happen."

"Yeah," she hiccupped, trembling, "no more outside, no more baseball, just dresses and curls."

It was months before Sally didn't feel that heavy body writhing against her skin in her sleep, biting, biting. Since then, she'd not been able to touch a page with a picture of a snake on it or watch a TV program about the creatures. She couldn't bear the cold, blank look in their eyes; it made her stomach quiver. If she saw a snake in the yard, her pulse hammered and her palms got sweaty. If she came upon one suddenly wriggling through the grass, her heart stuttered.

Ever since, Sally dreamt about snakes chasing her. She wouldn't allow a hand or foot to extend over the edge of the bed because she was sure there was one waiting to pull her into darkness. As she grew to adulthood, the terror subsided and she could go months without one of the dreaded dreams.

Lately she was having the dreams again and waking in the same clammy sweat. But now the snake wriggling in her shirt was much heavier, larger, and wrapped itself around her, squeezing her breath away.

Thump. The noise was against the bedroom door now, a bump and a dry, rustling, scraping sound. Sally dripped sweat, now wide awake and trembling. She thought she detected a musty, swamp smell. Thump, thump. She knew she'd have to open the door. I'm being silly, she chided herself; there was never anything there before. She took a deep breath and flung open the door.

Instinctively Sally knew this would be the last thing she'd ever see. Those black soulless eyes were level with her own, mesmerizing her. She froze. The patterned body, thick as her thigh, undulated slowly forward, coiled itself, and then struck, encasing Sally's slight form in a deadly grip. One scream-then she couldn't move her rib cage. As the giant muscles constricted, she heard her bones snap and she prayed for death.

CHAPTER II

"What do you think happened to her? I've never seen anything like that," said the police officer to his partner, who was looking sick and shocked.

"I don't know, but it's like someone put her in a giant vice and squeezed," his partner answered, swiping his arm across his sweaty forehead. "What was that slime all over her? And that smell? Phew!"

"Doc said it happened within the last half hour. If her neighbor hadn't been out walking his dog and heard her scream, we may not have found her for days. Looks like she lived here by herself."

The officers were standing under a massive old oak. High above them an enormous, richly patterned body quietly tightened its coils around a thick branch, making only a slight scraping sound. The cold ebony eyes flicked over the men below. Hunger gnawed at the giant body. *The small domestic cats and dogs just weren't enough lately. The woman would have kept the hunger abated for weeks*. It had just covered her with saliva and was about to swallow her when the sirens and banging of car doors started. Escape out of the house was through the cat door, the way it had come in. The distance to the nearby pond, where it had lived for several months since being discarded by its owners, was too far. Night hunting had been successful, except for tonight. The hunger grew.

CHAPTER III

Detective Carolyn White woke instantly. The sirens were close; she could hear them with the windows closed. The air conditioning clattered as it did when the weather was exceptionally humid, but she heard them. It sounded like they were coming right down the secluded, tree-lined road that wound past her condo. It was 11:00 on a steamy July night. There'd be complaints from those rich people at "the compound" again. The locals called it the compound, although the discreet sign at the gated front entrance said Ellington Estates. The village folks thought the place was a joke and the demanding inhabitants were a pain in the ass.

Carolyn rubbed her eyes and groaned as she pushed her long body out of bed. She overdid it at the gym today and was paying for it. She separated the mini blinds on the window. Sure enough squads heading toward the compound. Hopefully they hadn't been called out at this time of day for another missing pet.

Ellington Estates was completely screened from prying eyes. The whole property was fenced and on three sides thick forests of pine and cedar grew freely, giving year-round privacy. The houses had every convenience known to man. The grounds, with old oaks and pines, were cultivated to maintain a woodsy atmosphere. They even had a spring-fed pond, thick with cattails, seaweed, and monstrous imported koi- carp parading as goldfish. The thing that really tickled the local comedians was that the pond was heated to keep the water at bath temperature year round. The antics of the compound residents provided juicy tidbits of gossip at most of the local bars and pubs.

Carolyn smiled, stretching like a well-muscled, lean, and lanky greyhound. She figured she had enough time to brush her teeth and climb into a pair of jeans. She was tugging a brush through tangled, nut-brown hair when the call came.

"I'll be there in ten minutes," she said.

She frowned at the image of the striking, dark-eyed woman looking back at her from the mirror. She knew her elegant, sophisticated looks had much to do with getting her assigned to this unit. Captain Jerry Daniels, her boss, thought those good looks were what made her useful to the Lake View police force, not her brain or her skills as a detective. His condescending attitude never failed to bring out her stubborn, aggressive streak. One of the local good old boys and a veteran of twenty five years, the captain had no use for women cops. But he believed she spoke the language of the folks at the compound and could play peacemaker when they complained about every little thing, as was their habit. She knew he thought she was good for little else; her exemplary record at solving difficult crimes somehow escaped his notice.

Those same good looks forced her to work very hard to gain the respect and trust of her fellow officers - that and the fact her father had been a well respected Congressman, whose hobbyhorse had been corrupt cops. She never felt like she'd lived up to his expectations. Sometimes she wondered if, even though she loved her job, she'd become a cop just to annoy him. She clipped on her gun holster, checked her weapon, and grabbed her keys.

At the electronic gate, she recognized one of the officers who had patrolled this area at night for some years.

"What's going on, Bill," she said.

"It's the damndest thing, Detective," he said, his face ashen, pointing in the direction she was to take. "It's the big brown ranch house closest to the swamp." The electronic gates opened and she drove quickly through.

She always marveled at how hidden each of the houses were, even from one another. Privacy and seclusion had been the whole theme of Ellington Estates ten years ago when the developer first began the project. The lots had sold quickly and people moved from Chicago, fifty miles to the south.

The house she pulled up to was no longer hidden from view. Lights blazed inside and out as figures moved through the house and nearby brush.

"Hey Chet," she said, walking into the foyer through the open front door. Her eyes scanned the vast living room, missing nothing. A wall of glass faced the forest and a massive fireplace took up most of another. "What've you got?"

"Nasty," the short, stocky Sergeant said. "Follow me." He limped through an arch at the far side of the living room. He had been shot saving a child from a kidnapper some years earlier and his limp was more pronounced at the end of a long day.

They entered the sleeping quarters by way of a long, broad hallway. At the end of the hallway, where Carolyn judged the master bedroom to be, lay a small oddly shaped bundle that looked wet.

"Dear Lord," Carolyn sucked in her breath. On closer inspection, the bundle had a head and appeared to be female; though it was difficult to tell because the woman looked like she'd been through a compactor. "What is that smell?" Carolyn swallowed to keep from gagging.

"Do we know what happened to her Doc," she asked the small, scruffy man gently examining the body with rubber-gloved hands.

"I'll know more when I do the autopsy, but it's pretty evident she's been crushed," snapped Dr. Frank Jacobs. He hated odd cases. They always happened in the middle of the night. It was weird stuff like this that had convinced him to move from Chicago to the quiet of the country. "I'll have to have this viscous fluid she's covered with analyzed at the state lab. That'll probably take a couple days at best."

"What can you tell me now?" Carolyn asked quietly. It was hard to look directly at the victim. The expression of stark terror on the woman's misshapen face made the hair on the back of Carolyn's neck stand up.

"She was about five feet, maybe one hundred five pounds, very slightly built. I'd say between forty and fifty," he said, noting Carolyn's aversion to the body.

"The smell," Carolyn asked again, "Do you know what it is? It's like dead fish."

"Maybe it's coming from the swamp, the house is pretty close," Doc Jacobs said absently, all his attention on the body.

Leaving Doc Jacobs with the body, Carolyn began a slow circuit of the luxurious home. While she and Sergeant Adwell poked through each room, he filled her in on what he'd learned. The woman was Sally Donaldson, a divorcee, who lived alone with two cats, both of which were missing. According to Chet, Mrs. Donaldson's ex-husband was a well-known, well-liked, local contractor.

"The word is, Mrs. Donaldson was pleasant but a bit reclusive," Chet said.

"The ex?" Carolyn asked.

"His name is Sam Donaldson, mid forties, local guy, got a reputation for being tough to do business with."

"What do you mean?"

"He doesn't tolerate fools," Chet said going carefully through the desk drawers, "Some think he's a hard man. He owns a construction company that specializes in large luxury homes like these in the compound and office buildings. The company has a reputation for quality work."

"Did he get along with his ex-wife?"

"From everything I can get this early on, they got along okay. They've been divorced about ten years and have one daughter in college."

They entered the spacious living room where a tall, broad shouldered man stood watching two young officers outside searching the yard.

"Why don't you ask *me* how I get along with my ex-wife," the man said aggressively, turning to face them. "I'm Sam Donaldson. Where's Sally? The cops outside wouldn't tell me what's going on; just told me to wait here for Detective White."

"Mr. Donaldson," Carolyn said, extending her hand, "I'm Detective Carolyn White. Can we step outside? Our people haven't finished with the inside of the house yet." She walked toward the family room with its French doors. He followed her outside onto a spacious patio which would be charming in bright daylight, but looked surreal in the harsh, white glare of police spotlights. The nearby wooded area was ominous in the contrasting blackness.

"Can you tell me why you're here?" Carolyn said, watching his face closely. She sensed his agitation. He was keeping a tight rein on his self control.

"I was having a late dinner with friends around the corner and when I passed by I saw all the commotion. I came back to see what was going on," he said, his face tight, "Now I want to

9

know where Sally is."

CHAPTER IV

Jeremy Parker climbed out of bed just before first light. He was small for three years old, but his wiry little legs never stopped once he was moving. His mother and father slept soundly. They had been up late the night before because of the disturbance at the neighbor's house. They never heard him go down the back stairs and out the sliding door to the patio.

Jeremy's mind was on the bunny he'd seen a few days earlier, at the edge of the thick stand of trees and undergrowth that separated his house from the one next door. He'd seen the bunny when he'd been out in the yard with his mom. For several minutes they'd watched it, whispering to each other so as not to frighten it away.

His blue blankie picked up fresh cut grass as he dragged it behind him across the yard. The weak early morning light sparkled on the tiny medic alert bracelet he always wore. His mother, Jenny, said he couldn't take the bracelet off. It could keep him safe. The bracelet told the world he was asthmatic. He had trouble with the heavy, moist air on mornings like this. He wheezed slightly as he trundled closer to the still, dark woods.

Jeremy laughed softly. There at the edge of the woods, sitting under a large lilac bush was the plump bunny. The bunny hopped slowly to the other side of the bush, so intent on feeding that it never heard Jeremy's bare feet on the dewy grass. The rabbit never heard the soft rustle of a heavy body moving stealthily toward it through the tangled undergrowth either.

Ebony eyes set in a thick, flat, triangular head, stared without blinking as the boy came across the grass, closer and closer to the shrub. It had been focused on the rabbit when the house's door scraped open and the boy came out. Instinct relayed the message that the bright haired child would be easier to catch than the rabbit. The massive reptile slithered silently to the back of a neighboring spruce and waited.

No one heard Jeremy's final gasp as the heavy muscles constricted. Crouched in dense grasses and trembling in terror, the bunny watched the gigantic body thrash in the underbrush until the small prey was broken and lifeless.

Jenny Parker awoke with a start, the brilliant sunlight splashed across her soft face. They'd left the balcony curtains open the night before. She and Don had been trying to decipher what was going on at the neighbors' house. The thick trees had given them sporadic glimpses of squad cars with sirens wailing at one in the morning. Jenny listened carefully. No sound came from her son's room. Strange, Jeremy was an early bird and usually demanded his breakfast by this time. She smiled. Small as he was, her son would eat as many pancakes as kids twice his size.

"Okay, sleepy head," she murmured to her soundly sleeping spouse, "I'll get the coffee going." She smiled again as she tugged on her robe, thinking how much their golden-haired son looked like his golden-haired father, when they were sleeping. She moved quietly over to close the drapes so Don Parker could sleep a little longer. At the far end of the yard, near the woods, something blue caught her eye. It looked like a dirty rag. Recognition flickered for an instant in the back of her mind and then was gone. She quickly pulled on a light robe and hurried quietly downstairs to make the coffee, sure that her son was already up and hungry .

CHAPTER V

The sun slipped up past the horizon to warm the dew-splattered grass creating soft mists of pink and yellow. In a few hours it would be scorching. The beauty of the early morning was unnoticed by the two people standing close together talking in funeral parlor voices. Right then, at the edge of the swamp, everything was quiet, too quiet, even the birds weren't greeting the new day.

Carolyn shivered involuntarily when she realized where they were. The swamp, there would be snakes. She hated and feared snakes with a paralyzing intensity. Her father told her years earlier, impatient with her, if you look for snakes you won't see any. Carolyn remembered as a little girl walking into a circular, glass-walled room with her father. It was a special exhibit in a reptile garden, and an extra entrance fee was required. Small tropical trees touched the ceiling and dense shrubs were clustered in clumps of two or three. The air was thick, saturated, and hard to breathe. The guide had said to be sure and stay on the narrow stone path which wound around the trees and shrubs. She didn't notice anything right away because she was concentrating on the path. All of a sudden it hit her. Vibrant colors dripped from trees or lay in piles on the floor and some of them moved slowly, drowsy in the heat. Snakes; big ones, little ones, short ones, bright ones, dull ones were everywhere. She scanned the room quickly, jerking her head back and forth. Sweat beaded her brow, a scream stuck in the back of her throat. Frantically she looked over her shoulder at her father.

"If you make a scene, I'll never speak to you again," he hissed, red faced.

She put her head down, gulped a deep breath and looked only at the path immediately in front of her and made it through the room, sick and shaken.

Sam was unaware of her nervousness. He was trying to control his reaction to what he'd just seen and not let it invade his deepest self. He knew it would be intolerable if he couldn't put a lid on it. They had just come from the morgue. Unable to make himself enter Sally's house again, he and Carolyn had wandered toward the pond. Identifying what was left of his wife had been a gruesome experience. Sam fought to keep the bile down in his throat, it threatened to choke him. Sally had been crushed into an almost unrecognizable mound of human flesh, blood and bones.

"Are you alright?" he asked. Carolyn's beautiful face suddenly had a white, pinched look.

"Yes, I should be asking you that," she said nervously. "I have this stupid fear of snakes, and I just realized where we are."

"I don't like them much myself," he said. He was somewhat pleased that something could shake up this cool, efficient robot of a woman.

"Oh, this goes way beyond a normal distasteful reaction, it paralyses me," she replied, her voice shaking. "Let's walk down the road a bit."

They walked quietly for a few moments. Carolyn forced her mind back to the matter at hand. Could this man beside her, struggling to fight the pain and revulsion of what he'd just seen, have killed his wife? Could anyone put on such a convincing act as he was doing right now?

"You said you spent yesterday evening with friends nearby, how long were you with them?" she asked, turning her head to watch his face.

"You can't really believe I could have anything to do with Sally's death?" he said, his face flushing. "I realize that the ex-husband would be the first suspect, but that's outrageous. I could never do that to anyone, even someone I hated."

"Did you hate your ex-wife?" Carolyn asked softly, in an even, impersonal voice as she resumed walking down the road.

"Of course not," he sputtered, "Sally and I have known each other since first grade. We should never have married, but we caved-in to what everyone expected of us. It didn't work. We were both miserable."

"I'm sorry to have to ask you these questions now," she said coolly, "but you must realize because of the business you're in, you have equipment that could possibly crush someone as Sally was crushed." She'd stopped walking and turned to face him to better judge his reaction.

"You're crazy," he said, blue eyes blazing. He stared at her as if she were some kind of a monster.

Just at that moment, Sgt. Adwell drew up in a police car. "Detective White," he said, tensely, ignoring Sam Donaldson. "You're needed back at the house."

One look at his face and Carolyn knew Chet had something to say that upset him. "Mr. Donaldson, would you like a ride back to your car," she said, "I have no more questions for you just now."

Sam just grunted and slid into the back seat of the cruiser.

"Please make sure you don't leave town until this is all cleared up," Carolyn said crisply when they pulled up to Sally Donaldson's house. She saw the distaste in Sam Donaldson's eyes when he looked at her.

A bright yellow sports car careened into the driveway. A curly-headed, slight young woman spilled out of the car door. Sam Donaldson rushed to gather her in his arms, holding her tightly against his broad chest. She was sobbing. "Daddy, what happened, where is she? They wouldn't tell me anything, just that you wanted me home because something happened to Mom."

"You can't see her right now, let me take you home and I'll tell you all I know," he told her speaking as he would to a small child. He bundled her gently into the passenger seat of the little car and then struggled to fit his brawny frame behind the wheel.

Carolyn turned to face Sgt Adwell. "Well, Chet?"

"There's a couple wanting to talk to you, they live in the house next door. The two story log cabin. Their little boy has gone missing. There isn't a sign of him anywhere, no sign of a struggle, his bed was slept in, and the patio door was open. The only thing they found was the blue blanket he carried around with him. They found it at the far end of the yard by the woods between their property and Sally Donaldson's."

Carolyn looked thoughtfully at Chet, noting the concern in his eyes.

"And?" she said.

"It's just that there's too many odd things happening around here lately," he said slowly, mentally tallying events. "Last month there was the complaint someone was stealing the big goldfish from the Estate's pond. A couple weeks ago, there were several pets, dogs and cats, missing. Last night, Mrs. Donaldson was murdered and today the little Parker boy is missing. They don't seem to fit together, but..."

"Yes, I know," she said, "but my gut tells me they are all

connected somehow."

Don Parker answered the front door, his light blond hair tangled from sleep, a bewildered expression on his young face, like he'd been kicked in the stomach and didn't know why.

"I'm Detective White," Carolyn said kindly, "Sgt. Adwell said you wanted to see me. Your son is missing?" She hear soft sobs coming from somewhere in the house.

"Come in," Don Parker said, motioning them into the living room, "Let me get my wife."

"We don't want to disturb her," Carolyn said, the desperate whimpering sobs touched her, "if she's not up to it."

"No, I think it will be good for her, for both of us, to talk this out," Don said, "you see she blames herself for this. She blames both of us, but herself mostly."

"Poor woman," Chet Adwell said when the young man left the room. "So much worse when it's a child."

"What do you know about them?" Carolyn asked him, listening as the sobbing from the other room slowly subsided. She could hear the golden-haired young man speaking in soothing tones.

"Not a lot, they haven't been here long. Couple years I think," he said quietly. "They're from Chicago, wanted to live here to raise their boy away from the city and in a protected community. From all accounts they doted on the little fella."

Carolyn's breath caught in her throat when she looked at the haggard face of Jenny Parker. Even in distress, the woman was beautiful. She looked like a delicate flower with her pale blonde hair and soft blue-violet eyes.

"Mrs. Parker, I'm Detective White and this is Sgt. Adwell. We're looking into the disappearance of your son, Jeremy. That's his name, correct?"

"Yes," Jenny said, swallowing and breathing deeply in an effort to control herself, "Jeremy John."

"Can you tell me when you saw him last and when you noticed he was missing," Carolyn spoke gently. Jenny struggled to contain herself before she answered.

"I checked on him around one o'clock this morning. He has asthma, and this weather sometimes bothers him at night. I'm in the habit of poking my head in to make sure he's okay. He was sleeping quietly," she said softly. "This morning, we over-slept. We'd been up late because of the ruckus next door. I was so surprised that Jeremy wasn't up and hungry. When I checked his room his bed was empty. Then I found the sliding door to the patio open," her voice quivered. "I never heard anything, you'd have thought I would have heard someone in the house."

Don put his arm around his wife, pulling her closer to him on the couch. "I thought I locked that door, but I can't remember for sure. It's something I do automatically before we go to bed." He looked forlorn, his eyes begging them to understand.

Jenny rose and went to a small table in the corner of the room; she came back with a framed photo of a bright-haired, joyous-faced toddler. "This is the most recent picture we have of him," she said, offering it to Carolyn, clearly not wanting to give it up.

Jeremy stood looking into the camera, laughing, a small blue scrap of blanket clutched to his chest.

"I found his blankie by the woods," Jenny said, her voice

unnaturally deep in her effort to keep from breaking down. "He never went anywhere without it. He'd get hysterical if he didn't have it. I can't believe I didn't hear him." She hiccupped.

Carolyn knew Jenny Parker wouldn't be able to keep her composure much longer. "Have there been any strangers near the house or anyone paying Jeremy unusual attention lately?"

"No, nothing I can think of," Jenny looked anxiously at her husband.

"We keep a tight watch on Jeremy," Don said, "Anyone we don't know doesn't get close to him."

"I don't understand why anyone would do something like this," Jenny said, large tears flooding her eyes.

Carolyn stood. She knew they wouldn't get anything else useful from the Parkers at the moment. They were too upset, maybe later when they settled down a bit and had time to think about the events of the past couple days.

"Officers are already searching the woods, and we're bringing in a blood hound too. There will be other officers who will need to see Jeremy's room, please leave it as it is till they're done. They will be checking the rest of the house too, try not to disturb anything. I'll need to take the blanket with me, but I'll return it along with the picture as soon as I can." Carolyn knew she sounded cold and formal, but it was the only way she could bear the shattered look in Jenny Parker's eyes. "Please let me know immediately if you remember anything else," she said placing her and Sgt. Adwell's business cards on the coffee table.

"Well, what do you think," Carolyn asked her sergeant as they walked toward the police cruiser. It was now eight a.m. and she knew from experience it would be a long, long day.

"I told you there's odd stuff going on in the compound lately," he said unconsciously using the local name for the community. "That poor Mrs. Donaldson last night, just awful, and now this boy."

"Are you trying to tell me, you suspect some kind of satanic cult stuff, a serial killer, or some other crazy?"

"Well," he said and left it hanging in the air.

"It's okay Chet, because my thoughts are going in the same direction. Have you heard anything about any weird group in the area?"

"At the café yesterday morning, there was talk of drugs, people said it had to be someone high on drugs doing all this stuff." Chet swung himself behind the steering wheel, adjusted his holster and waited until she was settled in the patrol car. He turned to her and said with a grim smile, "Nobody's coming out here on a delivery, service call or much of anything else till this is cleared up."

The patrol car didn't even start to move when another cruiser raced up the driveway and skidded to a stop beside them.

"Detective, you're wanted at the swamp right away," the young officer squawked nervously, "Its old Mrs. Wittacker, she's dead."

CHAPTER VI

Mrs. Esther Wittacker tottered along the narrow asphalt road. Sometimes her skittish heart made her a little unsteady. She smiled wryly; she'd made it to her eighty seventh year, there had been times when the doctor didn't believe she'd last a half hour, but here she was. Esther left her cane at home this morning; she didn't use it when she felt strong. She resented the combination of arthritis and a heart condition, which on some days kept her house-bound. She usually knew what kind of weather they were going to have by mid-morning then she would decide if she was going out for her walk. Today she felt strong and breathed deeply of the heavy moist air. The hot summer sun soothed her aching shoulders. Occasionally she stumbled. Then she would pause, right herself, and go forward. This morning she decided to take the route that wound past the swamp.

As she walked she thought of the years she'd spent at Ellington Estates and wondered how much longer she'd be able to maintain her freedom. That depended on how long her daughter-in-law would let her live by herself. She dreaded the thought of a nursing home or one of those assisted living places. She wanted to be in her own house.

Esther cocked her head right then left. That was odd, there were no bird noises. Usually on a day like this they jabbered at each other and zoomed purposely from place to place. She tapped her hearing aids. They were working fine. Maybe there was a storm coming, birds got very quiet when a dangerous storm was coming. Her thoughts turned to the little missing boy. Word traveled fast in the gated community. How frightened his mother must be. Surely they would find him soon.

There was a soft whooshing sound and the tall bull rushes near the road separated as if it was parted by an invisible hand. She stood mesmerized, unable to move, when a thick triangular head broke the cover of the tall grass and came straight toward her. She'd never seen anything like it. The scream stuck in her throat. She whimpered like a small, frightened child.

"Ahhh," she uttered, as the monstrous creature came at her. Then suddenly it veered and slid into the murky waters of the swamp.

Her knees buckled, the world spun and it felt like a steel cable tightened around her rib cage. The last thing she saw was Sam Donaldson's concerned face bending over her. She tried to tell him what she had seen. She wanted him to know she thought the monster got the little boy. She wanted him to protect her. She didn't want it to get her. Esther Wittacker slipped into an unconsciousness from which she would never return, not knowing how much she relayed to Sam.

"Hurry, hurry," Sam entreated into his cell phone, "I think it's her heart. Dear God, I think she's dying." He held her in his arms, trying to will some of his abundant strength into that fragile body. *Esther, she had been so kind to him and Sally when they moved to the Estates as newlyweds years ago.* He gently took her pulse, and, as he feared she was gone.

Anger coursed through him. *What was going on here?* He wanted answers right now.
What was it Esther said? "Monster".

When Carolyn and Sergeant Chet Adwell reached the swamp, there was a group of people already gathered, speaking in hushed voices. Carolyn always wondered why people did that, it wasn't as if the dead person could hear them. She frowned when she noticed Sam Donaldson quietly standing near the group of police officers listening.

Sam knew he looked like a thunder cloud. Carolyn looked

over at him, frowned and took her officers aside to speak in soft guarded tones, which only frustrated Sam further.

"Okay Officer Jackson," she said to the most senior man in the group, "What's going on?" She motioned him to follow her and waved for Sgt. Adwell to tag along, "What's Mr. Donaldson doing here?"

"He's the one who found the body, except she was still alive when he found her."

"Will you ask Mr. Donaldson to join us," Carolyn said. "I'll want you to stick around and hear what he says. I want to know if it's the same story he told you before."

"Do you think it's strange that Mr. Donaldson's been around when a lot of these things have happened?" she asked Sgt. Adwell, after Officer Jackson walked toward Sam.

"I don't know, just coincidence, maybe."

"Detective White, Sgt. Adwell," Sam Donaldson said as he strode up, his face stormy.

"Tell me what happened here. You found the woman, but she wasn't dead when you found her?" Carolyn asked, seeing his eyes flash in anger.

"The woman, as you describe her, was Mrs. Esther Wittacker," he replied coldly. "I was driving slowly, looking for the little boy when I saw this bundle at the edge of the swamp. I came over to check it out. She was lying in a heap, muttering and clutching her chest. I called 911 and tried to make her comfortable. I thought it was probably a heart attack."

"What was she saying, Mr. Donaldson, could you make it out?" Carolyn sensed something more was bothering him.

"It didn't make any sense," Sam Donaldson said, clearly unhappy with what he was about to say. "She wasn't a fanciful person but she said she saw the monster. She got more agitated and yelled, the monster got the little boy. I couldn't get her to settle down. She died just as the ambulance pulled up." The anger drained out of his face and was replaced by a deep sadness.

"What do you think she meant by "the monster"? Carolyn asked, clearly surprised by this turn of events.

"I don't have the faintest idea," he said, getting angry all over again. There was something about Carolyn that set his teeth on edge. "You tell me just what the hell you think is going on here."

"We're working on it Mr. Donaldson," Carolyn said, putting out her hand to stop Sgt. Adwell who'd stepped forward at the tone in Sam's voice. "Please don't leave town without checking with me or Sgt. Adwell." Carolyn turned and walked away, motioning the sergeant to go with her.

CHAPTER VII

Later that evening Carolyn, lovely in a light cream-colored summer dress, with muted lighting softening her prominent cheekbones, sat across from her father in the town's best restaurant, The Purple Finch. Congressman Carleton White, smoothed back his perfectly groomed silver hair absently, wondering for the millionth time why his daughter insisted on being a cop and living in this rustic hole.

Carolyn had been telling him of the series of unusual happenings in Ellington Estates. As he listened her job and life style annoyed him even more than usual. *I'll have a talk with the Chief of Police and get her pulled off this case, this is no job for her. She should be married to the right man and giving me grandchildren.* He sniffed.

"I will never understand why you bury yourself in this backwater," he said for the umpteenth time, unable to restrain himself. "Now there's a serial killer on the loose and you're in the thick of it." He couldn't seem to stop himself, even though he knew it would start an argument. "You should be in Chicago living the life you were brought up for."

Carolyn's lips tightened, "Dad, I haven't seen you in two months, let's not argue." Disappointment and anger bubbled within her. When would he realize she was doing what she loved? When would he know she was her own person and would make her own decisions? She knew herself to be her father's daughter in her stubbornness.

Carleton's eyes widened and his nostrils flared, "Whose fault is it you haven't seen me in two months? I live in the same house and I'm quite sure you know your way there. It seems this precious job of yours is more important to you than I am."

Father and daughter glared at one another across the table. Carolyn felt tears of frustration at the edges of her eyes and she thrust out her jaw.

"Excuse me," she said getting up quickly and heading for the ladies' room. The tears flooded her eyes and she barely saw where she was going. She stumbled. Strong arms caught her and kept her from falling.

"I'm sorry," she said feeling like a clumsy fool. She blinked trying to clear her vision.

"You could hurt someone, charging through here like that," said a familiar stern voice.

Carolyn looked into Sam Donaldson's icy blue eyes. She felt as if she'd had cold water dashed in her face. She straightened, pulled away from his hands, and lifted her chin.

"I tripped," she said, her words clipped and succinct.

Later Sam would wonder if he really did see the pain in Carolyn's dark eyes before the cool arrogant look she gave him.

"Dad?" a soft voice questioned, then again "Dad."

"I'm sorry honey." Sam turned and smiled warmly at the slight young woman with him. She looked up at him sternly with a slight frown, waiting for him to introduce Carolyn.

He turned back to Carolyn, the soft look still on his face. "Detective White this is my daughter, Molly."

Carolyn smiled and nodded in acknowledgement.

"Detective White," Molly Donaldson said, in a determined voice, her eyes clear and blue like her father's. "I've been waiting to meet you. I'd like to speak with you, tomorrow if possible?"

"Yes, of course," Carolyn said, having completely regained her composure. "I should be in the office all morning. Stop by." She wondered if the daughter had something to say about her father's involvement in Sally Donaldson's death.

From where he sat, Sam Donaldson had a clear view of Carolyn's table. He saw Carleton's assessing look as Carolyn, head high and looking elegant, made her way back across the room. Sam noticed several men watch her walk to her table with interest. It was impossible not to notice the likeness between the beautiful young woman and the handsome, sophisticated older man. Her father or an uncle, Sam thought as he turned his attention to the menu, and not a happy relationship either. He unobtrusively watched the pair throughout the evening. It seemed the man alternated between lecturing Detective White and stony silences. Carolyn sat ramrod straight. A polite smile etched on her generous lips, she might have been made of marble. Occasionally he sensed her looking at their table, but when he looked, her eyes were elsewhere. He bent his head toward his diminutive daughter, who was again angrily going over what she knew of her mother's death and the lack of police action. Molly couldn't believe anyone could have a reason to harm Sally and she intended getting some answers from Detective White the following day.

Carolyn's casual glance at the father and daughter revealed Sam talking quietly and Molly's obvious agitation.

When Molly got home from dinner with her father she felt listless and drained. She curled up on a lounge chair on the patio. The humid heat of the day still hung like a shroud making it hard to breathe. The rustle in the tall weeds at the end of the yard, close to the swamp, didn't register as anything other than night noise. Although her mind unconsciously noted that it was too quiet, no frogs croaking or swamp insect noises. She looked carefully around the yard, squinting in the glare of the spotlights she'd turned on when she came outside. Molly didn't see the large mottled body surreptitiously slip through the tall grass just beyond the spotlight's reach. What she and her father talked about at dinner ran through her mind. He had argued with her about staying in her mother's house, but she had insisted. Although she'd spent time with her father after the divorce, it was her mother's house she considered home. Molly didn't believe herself to be a fanciful person, but she felt closer to her mother here. At times throughout the day, she thought her mother was trying to tell her something. Suddenly Molly felt uneasy, like someone was watching her. She let her gaze travel over the now silent yard and realized the swamp noises had stopped. *Where were the voices of the frogs, crickets and other night insects?*

It was growing hungry again and needed to feed soon. The unblinking obsidian eyes watched as the small young woman moved restlessly on the lounge chair. Its tongue darted in and out testing the air, nostrils wide open it breathed softly. There was a large expanse of brightly lit lawn between it and the girl. It waited patiently, speed wasn't its forte. It needed the prey to come to it. It silently coiled the massive muscles in preparation for an attack and settled, willing the young woman to come out into the yard toward it.

Molly shivered, goose bumps creeping up her spine. She imagined someone, something in the darkness just beyond the floodlights glare. *This is silly, I'm just scaring myself.* As she was getting up from the lounge chair, the phone rang. She went quickly into the house locking the sliding door behind her. The cat door caught her eye and she slid the lock on it shut too. As she reached for the phone it stopped ringing and the answering machine picked up.

"Molly, its Dad. Please pick-up. I need to know you're okay staying in that house." Sam said, pacing back and forth across his living room. The sound of Molly's voice when she picked up made his knees weak.

"Hey Dad," Molly said softly, watching the yard through the sliding door.

Sam heard something in her voice that made the hair on the back of his neck stand up. "What's wrong Molly girl," he said, keeping his voice gentle and controlled.

"It's probably just me, I've got the jitters I guess. I was just sitting out on the patio and it felt like someone was watching me," she said, now moving from room to room turning on lights.

"I'm coming over there."

"No Dad," Molly said, trying to sound exasperated. She didn't want him to know how foolish she felt letting herself get spooked, thinking someone was watching her. She acknowledged to herself that his strong voice on the phone was just what she needed to hear to pull herself together.

"I locked all the doors and windows, even the cat door," she said smiling, wondering how anyone would get through that little swinging door. "I'm going to get into my p.j.s and crawl into bed. I'm beat." Maybe it had been foolish to insist on staying in this house so soon, she thought, although she didn't feel afraid.

"How about I pick you up for breakfast around eight," Sam said, relieved at hearing the normal tone back in her voice.

CHAPTER VIII

Molly slept deeply. Somewhere in her subconscious she heard the thump, thump against the cat door, but it wasn't loud enough to bring her out of the sound sleep.

"Rough night?" Sam said noting the dark circles under his daughter's blue eyes the next morning.

"I slept hard, but I seemed to hear pounding, faintly like it was coming from far away," Molly said musingly, not able to fully pull the memory from her mind. "I want to go see Detective White right after breakfast; I want to know what's going on."

Sam smiled at Molly's determined face. It relieved him not to hear that frightened tone in her voice. "Yes dear," he said meekly, mischief dancing in his eyes.

"Mr. and Ms Donaldson to see you Detective," Sergeant Adwell announced from the doorway of Carolyn's office, a short time later. Carolyn was irritated; she'd been on the phone for almost an hour with the state lab and knew little more now than she did when she got to work at seven. She rose from her desk chair as Molly and Sam entered her office.

Usually she moved visitors to the couch and chairs by the large window, it was informal and comfortable. However, today she preferred keeping the desk between her and the Donaldsons. It put control of the meeting in her hands and kept it official. She waved them to the chairs in front of her desk, said good morning and shook their hands.

"How can I help you today?" Carolyn began, a friendly smile on her face. She carefully looked at Sam to see if she could tell if he'd noticed much of the exchange between her and her father the night before.

"This is the second day since my mother's murder," Molly began firmly, her small pointed chin stuck out as if she expected to be slugged. "I want to know what you're doing and why you haven't arrested anyone."

Carolyn was impressed. It wasn't everyone Molly's age who could be indignant with a police officer. Perhaps because I'm a woman, Carolyn mused for an instant. *Would Molly be as aggressive if the case were being handled by a male officer.*

Sam saw Carolyn's professional face replace the warm friendly smile with which she'd welcomed them. He was surprisingly disappointed. He let his daughter go ahead because he knew Molly needed to do this for her own welfare. She was like him, she couldn't sit around and wait for things to happen, she tried to take the bull by the horns and get something done.

"We really only have one possible suspect at the moment, Ms Donaldson," Carolyn said quietly watching her visitors. Unbeknownst to them she pressed a small button under the top of her desk. Now they were being recorded; audio and video.

Both Sam and Molly leaned forward in their chairs.

"Who's that?" Molly demanded.

"Your father," Carolyn said coolly, watching the pair.

"Are you nuts!" Molly sputtered. "You can't be serious. My Mom and Dad were divorced but they still cared about each other."

Cold rage from Sam. "It's okay Molly," he said through tight lips, his hard eyes on Carolyn. "The husband is always the first suspect, especially the ex-husband, no matter how well the couple got along. Isn't that right Detective?"

Carolyn gave a half smile. "It is a documented fact, most victims are murdered by people they know and, more often than not, by their spouses."

"Tell me Detective," Sam said, the last word spat like a bad taste in his mouth, "what crushed Sally and what was that nasty slime she was covered with?"

Molly flinched at the visual Sam's words evoked. She shook her head trying to remove the picture in her mind's eye. Sam reached over and took her hand.

"We haven't gotten the report back from the state crime lab yet. I expected it this morning. They're having a little bit of trouble with the viscous substance which covered the body. As far as what crushed Mrs. Donaldson, perhaps you can answer that yourself, Mr. Donaldson. You do own heavy equipment."

"I wondered how long it would be before someone openly said that and since I have heavy equipment, I must have killed my wife." Color stained Sam's cheeks, his eyes were like stony blue pebbles.

Molly's face took on a pinched, confused expression. Carolyn saw it had never even crossed Molly's mind that her father could be responsible for her mother's death.

"That's sick," Molly said, going quickly from shock to anger. "My parents worked hard at keeping up a good relationship. Neither one wanted a bitter divorce. My Dad always did whatever he could to make my Mom's life easier."

"Okay, honey, okay," Sam said gently, letting go of her hand and putting his arm around Molly's shoulders.

"It's not okay," Molly said. "They don't know anything about how well you and Mom got along and apparently haven't taken the time to find out."

"I think you have your answer to where the police are with this investigation," Sam said to his daughter, and gave Carolyn a hard look. "I think we've taken enough of Detective White's time. Since she's convinced that I'm guilty of your mother's death, maybe she needs the time to look for that little boy, or find out what scared Mrs. Wittacker into a heart attack."

"But Dad," Molly started, her curls quivering in her agitation.

"No buts, let's get out of here." Sam pulled his daughter to her feet and moved her to the door. He looked over his shoulder at Carolyn. "Unless I'm under arrest that is." He paused a moment and then gently pushed his daughter out the door.

Carolyn watched as they moved down the hall. Sam put his arm around Molly and pulled her close talking to her earnestly. At that moment Carolyn envied Molly. Carleton White had certainly never treated his daughter with such loving care. She sighed and reached for her car keys. She wanted to take another look at the spot Mrs. Whittaker died.

CHAPTER IX

There was a musty, heavy smell to the air as she got closer to the swamp. It was too hot. The sun was blindingly bright. Carolyn could feel the familiar headache beginning behind her eyes, the usual aftermath of an evening spent in her father's company. She was surprised to see Sam Donaldson's truck near the cordoned off area where Mrs. Whittaker collapsed. He was standing near the bull rushes at the edge of the swamp, looking at something so intently he didn't hear her approach. He squatted down to take a better look.

"Is there something we missed, Mr. Donaldson," Carolyn said, a slight edge to her voice.

"I don't know if you missed it or not since I'm not privy to your investigation," Sam said coolly. "But here's a tunnel-like path that seems to come out of the pond itself and ends here near the road, close to where Mrs. Whittaker fell."

Carolyn kneeled down next to him, automatically taking a pair of rubber gloves from her pocket and pulling them over her long elegant fingers. "It just looks like an animal trail, muskrat, something like that," she said, very aware of Sam's nearness.

"Yes, perhaps," Sam said, standing up, her light perfume filling his nostrils. "I just wanted to see if there was something out of the ordinary about this place. Something I might not have noticed because I was so busy with Mrs. Whittaker."

Sam began to walk toward his truck, Carolyn hesitated, pulling off the rubber gloves and then followed him.

"Mr. Donaldson," she began, she was tempted to tell him about the preliminary specimen report she'd received from the state lab just after he left her office that morning. Something made her hesitate and she heard herself saying, "Where can we find you if we need to?"

"I'll be at my office," he said disgustedly, "I'm not going anywhere till this is all cleared up." He slammed the pickup's door hard enough to make the cab rock and the gravel spit as he stomped on the gas.

Carolyn walked thoughtfully back to the grass tunnel, squatted down and peered up it. She didn't really believe as did Sgt. Adwell, that Sam Donaldson killed his wife. She knew he could have killed her before the late dinner with his friends. *But what about the crushed body? What about the preliminary specimen report that the slime covering Sally Donaldson's body didn't come from a local source?* The state lab was still working on the specimen. The whole thing was taking on a bizarre tone. Carolyn had been absently staring at the swamp, lost in her own thoughts. She shivered in the hot morning sun a chill raising goose bumps on her arms. Suddenly she had an overwhelming urge to run. Where were the usual sounds, the birds, the insects; it was too quiet. The swamp water, so still and stagnant seconds ago, rippled violently, then was smooth again. Carolyn shook herself, looking around carefully trying to discover the source of the menace in the air. She walked quickly to her jeep. Not until she was driving away did the sense of danger leave her.

It lay near the edge of the swamp, lethargic in the hot sun. It had been aware of the man and woman, had watched them languidly. Somewhere in its drowsy brain, it knew the two of them represented a danger, but it also knew it could slip into the black water at the slightest movement it its direction. The slam of the truck door was loud enough to awaken it fully. The woman was alone crouched down by the edge of the pond directly across from it. Silently it slipped into the water. It was always hungry these days. Soon it would have to feed again.

CHAPTER X

"Yes, yes I'll go," Carolyn said to her boss the following day. She had spent the afternoon with sweat dribbling down her back because the ancient air-conditioning in the office was barely limping along in the muggy Wisconsin summer heat. Now she had to attend a cocktail party given by the mayor's wife, in Captain Daniel's place, when all she wanted was a cool shower, a beer and some mindless television. She'd gone over every facet of the events of the last three days. She knew that they somehow fit together, but couldn't find the tie that bound them.

By seven that evening, in a slightly better frame of mind after a cold shower, a beer and a twenty minute nap, Carolyn pulled up to the Mayor's home on the opposite side of the lake from the compound.

She moved through the knots of guests pretending to be unaware of the silences which followed her and then the quick whispered comments about the compound case. The trim white summer sheath she wore accented her golden tan, contoured arms and long, shapely legs. Carolyn moved with the ease of one accustomed to attending social gatherings, nodding at people she knew. She headed purposely for Mary Ellen, Mayor Scott's wife, to make her boss's apologies for not coming himself.

"Well how are you, Carolyn," Mary Ellen said with genuine warmth, she liked this attractive, intelligent young woman.

"I'm well thank you Mrs. Scott," Carolyn replied. She was always comfortable with Mary Ellen on the rare occasions they met. "I'm afraid you're stuck with me tonight instead of Chief Daniels, he sends his regrets. He had a meeting with the governor in Madison."

"Yes, I know, my husband's on his way there too. There's a lot of ruckus being stirred up about the compound. Let's get you a drink, I'll bet you could use one." The low murmur of voices and soft laughter had resumed throughout the beautiful room. As long as Carolyn was with Mary Ellen, everyone was careful to appear charming and normal.

CHAPTER XI

Thirteen-year-old Abby Petersen hurried along the twilight lit path, which skirted the swamp and wound through the old oaks and dense undergrowth. She was figuring out how she was going to cover up the hickey Brian Messing had given her before her father saw it. Her dad told her she wasn't old enough to see boys, especially Brian who was sixteen. Brian had picked her up from her friend Janey's house early and they'd spent some time necking in his old truck. He'd dropped her off at the mouth of the trail because she didn't want her dad to see Brian drive her home. As the light faded Abby's excitement turned to anxiety, the events in the compound the last couple days suddenly crowding her thoughts. Her father had warned her not to take any of the paths through the woods until whatever was going on was settled. She glanced behind her at a slight rustling sound in the tall grass. Her foot caught a knurled root which crossed the path. She went down hard hitting her head on the solidly packed trail. She lay there a minute, stunned and trying to clear her vision. Some sense of self preservation jerked her to a sitting position, but it was already too late.

Abby started to stand when the powerful jaws grabbed her arm in a vice-like grip. Crack! The bone snapped and she was thrown screaming to the ground. Massive, beautifully marked coils encased her slight body, crushing her windpipe and covering her mouth and nose before she could do more than give a whimper. Her small, red, heart-shaped purse had been flung, at impact, behind a clump of bushes. The large body writhed with its contractions, rolling over and over smashing the dense undergrowth. There, in a little while all was silent again. It unhinged its jaws and began to swallow the saliva-covered mass that had been Abby Petersen.

Hours later Harold Petersen frantically called the police.

"She was supposed to come straight home from Janey Elbert's house," he told the police officer, "but now I find out that Brian Messing picked her up early in his truck. I called his house but there's no answer."

CHAPTER XII

Sam Donaldson watched Carolyn move across the room toward Mary Ellen Scott. He admired the composed smile on her face, the way she pleasantly greeted friends even though he knew she heard the sharp comments about her handling the compound events. In spite of himself he liked her classy style. He was surprised to find how annoyed he was with the negative whispers going on around him. Slowly, he began to make his way to where Carolyn spoke quietly with the mayor's wife.

"Carolyn," Mary Ellen said, seeing Sam approach, "I'd like to introduce you to Sam Donaldson."

Carolyn turned as Mary Ellen spoke and said, "I'm acquainted with Mr. Donaldson."

"Of course," Mary Ellen said, flustered, "you would be."

Carolyn mentally prepared herself for a confrontation, although her face betrayed nothing of her consternation. She was surprised at Sam Donaldson's greeting.

Sam extended his hand to Carolyn with a warm "Hello Detective." Then he turned to Mary Ellen.

"Yes, Detective White is in charge of the investigation into Sally's death, and doing a good job too," Sam said, speaking a bit loudly and looking around at the avid expressions on the faces of people nearby. Those that noted his glance were suddenly embarrassed and started conversations which had nothing to do with the recent events at the compound.

Mary Ellen smiled charmingly and asked about Molly, apparently she and Sam were old friends and this was a way to normalize the conversation. After pleasantries were exchanged, Mary Ellen excused herself to greet late arrivals, leaving Sam and Carolyn by themselves.

Sam took Carolyn's arm and said again loud enough for those people close by to hear, "Let me get you another drink, there's something I want to talk with you about." He guided her to a quiet corner, taking two glasses of white wine from a passing waiter.

"I hate the wine they serve at these things," he said with a smile. To the casual observer it would appear that he was making a pleasant comment to her.

"Me too," Carolyn said, following his lead, and smiling broadly as if he'd said something amusing. She noted conversations were resuming a normal flow about politics, what the pastor said on Sunday and what little Johnny was up to now. She breathed a sigh of relief.

"Whew," Carolyn said, "Thank you for heading off the dogs."

"You're welcome," he said and then on impulse, "You want to blow this joint and get a beer?" *Why had he said that with the phony Bogart accent?*

"You bet," Carolyn said grinning, suddenly feeling light-hearted for the first time since this case started.

Sam clenched his jaw to keep it from dropping. *A real smile makes her look like another person.* He had asked her on impulse because he was irritated with the poor behavior of the people around them. He never really thought she'd accept. They made arrangements to meet at Burt's Bar, a small place at the edge of town, where Sam was well known and comfortable.

Carolyn startled herself by accepting his invitation and she knew the chief would probably frown, but she could say she was hoping he'd say something to incriminate himself. She'd been dampening down the attraction she'd felt for this man soon after they'd first met. She liked his air of command and quiet self-confidence. *Sure wasn't good police procedure to get involved with your number one suspect.*

They took a back booth at Burt's.

"Just for tonight, let's take a break from Sally's murder and all the weird stuff going on at the compound," Sam said, when they'd ordered a couple of beers. He'd been taken aback to hear Burt greet Carolyn as a well-known and well-liked customer. Sam marveled at the beautiful face across the table from him. He wondered why he hadn't noticed before what a striking woman Carolyn was. He liked the way the subdued lighting brought out the red highlights in her hair. He couldn't believe he was wondering what it would feel like to run his hand slowly down her silky cheek. Sam mentally shook himself.

Carolyn smiled at him. "Thank you," she said, "there's nothing I'd like better than to not think about this case tonight."

"Molly appears to be a determined young woman," Carolyn said, thinking this would be safe ground. She liked looking at this man. His broad chest and shoulders and apparent strength made her feel safe. That was an odd thought when she was the one who carried the gun. Such a strange sensation for someone who'd always depended on no one but herself. She'd never found anyone she felt trustworthy enough to handle things that pertained to her personally. She sighed deeply, leaned back into the worn old leather of the booth and began to relax.

"She is that," Sam smiled, thinking of his strong-minded

daughter. "She has all the aggressiveness of a twenty year old storm trooper. Although she spooked me last night."

"Oh, how," Carolyn asked, a flutter of dread in the pit of her stomach.

"She insisted on staying at Sally's and when I called to check on her; she said she had the feeling someone was watching her. But then she claimed she was being silly and didn't want me to come over there. Of course I did. I parked down the road a bit and took a walk around the house and found nothing. So I sat in my truck and just watched the house for most of the night."

"Murder sites are often creepy for a long time," Carolyn said trying to alleviate his concern and still the unease creeping down her spine.

"I'm sorry" Sam said, "we weren't going to talk about this and here I started it. Tell me how you came to be a cop here, when you're so obviously too sophisticated for this job?"

Carolyn laughed. "You've got the wrong slant. I like it here. I do come from a different world, my father is a congressman. I grew up in DC with that lifestyle. When I went to the police academy I was buddies with someone from a small town in Wisconsin. I was enchanted with his stories about his life growing up there. So when this job opened up, I jumped at the chance. I've had few regrets."

"Your folks okay with you're being a small town cop?" Sam asked although he was pretty sure he knew the answer.

"My mother has never been happy with my becoming a police officer and my father believes I've betrayed my upbringing. He thinks I should have married a politician on his way to becoming president or something. He would have been happier with a son to follow in his footsteps. I've long since accepted that."

Right, Sam thought, that's why he brought you to tears the other night in the restaurant.

"Are you an only child?"

"Yes, it's hard on them; they put all their eggs in one basket."

"And you," Carolyn asked. "You grew up here?"

"Yes I did, but Sally was from California. We were in kindergarten and first grade together but then her folks moved to LA. Our parents kept up their relationship during our growing up years and we saw one another a couple times a year. We went to the same college. She had a hard time with small town Wisconsin at first."

"And your daughter? Will she stay here?"

"Molly loves it here. We had to fight with her to go away to school. I sometimes think she thought she could fix things between her mother and me."

"That's what a lot of kids think when they're parents are divorced, I know I did," Carolyn said.

"Don't get the wrong impression, Sally and I just lost each other along the way, but we stayed friends. Maybe that's all we were ever really meant to be," Sam said, moving his beer glass in circles on the table.

Sally had to restrain herself from reaching across and taking his hand. Instead she said, "I think I have to call it a night. Thanks for the beer."

Sam took her arm and walked her to her jeep. He felt an electrical charge when he touched her. "I'd like to do this again," he said and bent to kiss her cheek.

"Yes, me too, when all this is done."

Then he kissed her mouth, lightly, softly, warmly. Her knees wobbled.

Sam turned without another word and headed for his truck. He got in and waited until she drove away. His heart hammered. Such a slight kiss, he could still feel her soft mouth. He wanted this woman, but he knew he'd have to wait until the killer was caught and he was completely cleared.

Carolyn fell into a restless sleep. Erotic images of her and Sam danced through her mind. She shoved off her covers, too hot. She squirmed with longing as the images became more explicit. The phone's shrill ring jarred her awake. She fumbled to pick it up. One o'clock in the morning.

"Lt. White," she said huskily, and then "I'm on my way."

CHAPTER XIII

Molly tossed and turned in her mother's bed. Thump, thump, she dimly heard the pounding through the mists of sleep. *What was that noise?* Her mind stumbled back toward oblivion. Thump, thump. Now she was wide awake. Thump, thump it came again pounding on something in the house. Molly got up, opened the bedroom door and started down the dark hallway. Something made her retrace her steps to the end of the hall where she flicked the light switch. The light made her bolder. Thump, thump. Molly stopped, she crept down the hallway slowly, stomach knotted.

At the end of the hallway she rounded the corner into the family room. The French doors were dark; she'd forgotten to turn on the patio lights. Something moved in the darkness outside, something big. Molly froze. It seemed an eternity before she could move again. *What made her think she could stay in this house?* She took deep breaths working up her nerve. Molly took giant steps stretching her legs as far as they would go to cross the family room quickly to the patio light switch. White light shattered the darkness like a sword slashing through evil.

There was nothing on the patio, but the dew covered grass on one side was flattened as if something heavy had lain on it. Out by the edge of the swamp the tall reeds and swamp grass moved violently although there was no wind. Molly shivered. Something bumped her bare foot. She sucked in a breath to scream and looked down. There at the side of the French doors the small cat door swung back and forth on one hinge. It bumped into her foot again. *It was fine when I checked it when I went to bed. What happened? Oh, Lord something was trying to get in!* She frantically looked about her for something to hold that door in place. In the end she used encyclopedias from the bookcase nearby to block the cat door. She rushed to the bedroom and grabbed her cell phone from the bedside table. *Please let him answer, please!!*

"Dad, Dad, I'm scared!" Molly whimpered when her father answered.

Sam Donaldson was in his truck and on the road in less than two minutes. He drove as if a madman were chasing him. Molly's terrified voice echoing in his head, *Dad, Dad*. He used his cell to call 911 explained the situation, demanded a squad and requested Detective White be notified.

Eight minutes later he skidded into his late wife's driveway. Leaving the truck lights on he jumped out of the truck and reached back in for his 300 Winchester Magnum rifle and a loaded clip. He slammed the clip into the rifle and headed toward the front door. Molly opened the door and her father gathered her close with one arm. He stepped inside locking the door behind him. Molly was trembling.

"You okay?" Sam said searching her face.

"Dad," she stammered, "something was out there. It tried to get in the cat door."

"Whoa Babe, slow down and tell me what happened." Sam began walking toward the family room off the kitchen. He pushed Molly behind him, told her to talk softly and clicked off the safety on his rifle. In a whisper she told him what happened and begged him to be careful.

Just as Sam was looking at the broken cat door, the front doorbell rang. Molly jumped at the sound.

"Probably the cops," Sam said, "but to be safe, look through the peep hole before you open that door."

Carolyn stood on the step, that uneasy feeling in the pit of her stomach again. She had a sense of foreboding. The instant she saw Molly as the door opened she exhaled the breath she didn't realize she'd been holding.

"Thank God you're okay," she said. "The squad's right behind me. Where's your Dad?"

"This way," Molly whispered. Gone was the aggressive young woman who had demanded information about her mother's death and in her place was this white-faced, frightened girl who looked about to collapse. Molly surprised Carolyn by taking her hand, with a hand as cold as a grave, and leading her toward the family room.

Sam was kneeling beside a small, top-hinged door at floor level next to the French doors in the family room. The little door, though bolted at the bottom, was tilted awkwardly. Upon closer inspection the hinge was pulled loose from the frame and swaying slightly. Molly had been filling Carolyn in with a half whispered voice which put everything in crystal sharp reality.

Carolyn unsnapped the strap which held her revolver in its holster and reached for the door handle.

"What are you doing?" Sam said rising as if to try to stop her. "You're not going out there by yourself." Suddenly he was angry; she was taking a foolish chance.

"My job," Carolyn said, raising a hand to stop him from following her outside. "Stay here with Molly. I assume the rifle's loaded."

"The squad will be here in a minute, you need to stay in case he comes back and I miss him," Carolyn said in a voice that brooked no argument.

Sam looked down at his daughter and then back at Carolyn, clearly frustrated by not being able to protect both of them. "Be careful."

Carolyn nodded, scanned the now well lit back yard and then stepped outside. After again scanning the yard she bent to look at the outside of the cat door. There were bloody smears on the door and she kept getting an odd smell. *That smell, where had she run across it before?* She walked across the patio toward the area of flattened grass. It looked like something had been dragged across it, wiping up the heavy dew as it went. The humid summer air felt almost too wet to breath, and everything was absolutely still. There weren't even any night noises. It was if all the little creatures of the swamp and woods were holding their collective breath and waiting for something to happen, deadly quiet.

She was halfway across the yard walking carefully alongside the flattened grassy area when the shriek of sirens split the stillness like a banshee scream. She surveyed the yard again paying close attention to where it butted against the tall swamp grass and the woods nearby, and then she turned and retraced her steps.

Sgt. Chet Adwell waited on the patio for her. She briefly told him what happened and asked who else was there.

"Just me, everyone else was tied up, but they'll be here as soon as they can."

"Okay, be prepared for anything and let's follow this flattened grass trail. Let's see if we can find out who made it." She took the lead back across the yard as the Sergeant drew his weapon.

When they reached the edge of the yard they split up, Carolyn took the perimeter of the yard closest to the swamp and Sergeant Adwell took the opposite direction which skirted the woods. They were some distance apart when he heard a slight rustling in the woods. He undid the safety on his revolver and stepped into the woods. At that instant some instinct made Carolyn turn and look for her Sergeant. She saw him enter the woods with his gun drawn. Carolyn ran toward where Sergeant Adwell entered the woods.

Sam, standing at the French doors saw all the action as if it was a silent movie. The doorbell rang and he sent Molly to answer it. "It's more police," she yelled. Sam half ran to the front door and began to tell two officers as quickly as possible about the night's events and what was happening at the moment. Some of the officers began running around the outside of the house, toward the back yard, drawing their weapons.

Its head hurt. Its face was cut and bleeding. It had felt the little door giving away under its hammering when it sensed movement in the house. Its instinct warned of danger and it moved its large body quickly across the wet grass toward the woods. Primitive anger seared its brain. The yard was flooded in brilliant light just as it moved into the woods where it hid in a nearby thicket. It was hungry and very, very angry. Soon there was movement at the edge of the woods. A small man. He was coming into the woods.

Carolyn had almost reached the spot where she had seen Chet enter the woods when she heard his horrible guttural scream: a gunshot and then silence. Without a thought for her own safety she stepped forward into the woods. After a few steps she saw movement in a nearby thicket. She raised her weapon and advanced. Behind her she could hear the other officers racing across the yard. On the ground she saw Chet's out flung arm. A bit further away the undergrowth snapped as if someone was running quickly through it. "Stop or I'll shoot!" Carolyn fired.

It moved quickly through the undergrowth toward the pond. It slipped into the murky night darkened waters and hid among the tall cattails and rushes. Now it became absolutely still and waited.

Sam, heart in his throat, raced across the yard. One officer was talking excitedly on his cell phone, giving directions. He found Carolyn kneeling beside an unconscious Sergeant. His anxious glance swept over her body. No wounds. He knelt beside her.

"My God, how did that happen?" Sam said at the sight of Sergeant Adwell's mauled leg from which blood was pumping at an alarming rate.

"Give me your belt for a tourniquet. I've got to stop this bleeding! He'll bleed out before the rescue squad gets here," said Carolyn. Sam quickly stripped off his belt; trading places with Carolyn to apply pressure on the wound while she deftly wrapped the belt around the sergeant's thigh.

Sam raced back across the lawn shouting to Molly, who had come out on the patio, "Get me a blanket, hurry!" Molly ducked back into the house and was just coming back out when Sam reached her. "Watch for the rescue squad, send them back to the woods." Sam yelled as he raced back to the fallen officer unfolding the blanket as he went.

"Here let me put this over him, it'll help with shock. My God he's lost a lot of blood, must be a torn artery."

"Thanks," Carolyn said, glancing at Sam as he gently wrapped the blanket around the too still form.

Sam's chest tightened at the sight of pain flooding Carolyn's eyes. She quickly ducked her head and attended to what she's was doing.

"Where the hell is that squad," she said desperately. Looking up again as a young policeman approached.

"Detective," the young officer who'd been on the phone said, "The squad's on its way. I'll head to the front of the house and send them back here." He cast a worried look as Carolyn held Sam's belt tightly around the slashed leg of his unconscious Sergeant. The crimson stream had slowed. In the distance sirens wailed and the officer turned and bolted across the lawn.

Hours later Carolyn sat slumped in the hospital waiting room, her clothes stiff with Sergeant Adwell's blood. She and several of his fellow officers had donated blood as the Sergeant was perilously close to death when they finally reached the emergency room. Sam sat next to her, even though she'd told him to go home. Secretly she was glad he was there. She couldn't get Sergeant Adwell's ashen face out of her mind.

"I don't think I can stand it if he doesn't make it," she said quietly. "He was always there to back me up. Especially when I first got here and was having problems with some of the others who didn't like having a woman cop on their force. He eased the way for me."

Sam wanted to take her in his arms and comfort her, but he knew she wouldn't appreciate that especially in front of her officers who kept coming and going giving her reports from their search of the surrounding woods and pond. The only thing they'd found was small traces of blood on some leaves a short distance away from the thicket where Sergeant Adwell was found.

"Detective White," said a doctor coming through the doors that lead to the surgical area. Carolyn and Sam both stood up and the officers who'd been standing talking in low tones stopped speaking.

"Sergeant Adwell is in the critical care recovery room. We're going to keep him there for a while, he's not out of the woods yet. The surgery went as well as can be expected. There were a lot of torn blood vessels. They were repaired, but he's very weak from blood loss and there's no sign of consciousness yet. Do you know how he got this wound?"

"Not yet, but I believe we're getting closer. Can I see him?" Carolyn said, desperate to make sure with her own eyes her sergeant was alive.

"For just a couple minutes."

She stood at his bedside staring intently at the grey face before her. Carolyn knew the police force was the only real family the sergeant had. She took his cold hand in her own warm ones, willing her strength to somehow flow into his body. "Come back Chet, we need you," she whispered, a tear slipping slowly down her cheek. The nurse came in and softly touched Carolyn's arm signaling her time was up.

"Please call me, the moment there's any change," Carolyn said as she handed the nurse her card with her home phone number written on the back. Suddenly the night was catching up with her and she was exhausted.

"You need to get some sleep," Sam said as he walked her back to her jeep. "You're not any good to anyone in this condition." He wanted to bundle her up, take her home and keep her safe.

"I'm just going to stop by the office and see if there's anything from the state lab yet, then I'll get some sleep."

"Have dinner with Molly and me tonight? Nothing fancy, just simple and quiet."

"I'd like that," Carolyn said looking up into his anxious eyes.

She had been about to refuse, but the concern in his voice touched her and she liked this man better than anyone she'd met in a long time.

By the time she reached the station it was eight a.m. She wanted a meeting with the men who'd been on the call last night. She needed to pick their brains for thoughts and opinions.

Two hours later she let herself into her condo, bone weary. She stripped off her clothes leaving them where they fell and climbed into bed. Almost immediately she fell into a deep sleep barely moving for the next couple of hours. Something nagging at the back of her mind made her toss and turn. She was half awake when her cell phone rang.

CHAPTER XIV

"Detective, we've received the final specimen report back, it's kinda strange," said Officer Bell.

"Read it to me," Carolyn demanded, grabbing her robe and heading for the shower, her mind sluggish. "What?" she said, not believing her ears. "I'm jumping in the shower and I'll be there in half an hour."

Within twenty minutes she was showered, had coffee in her travel mug, and was on the way to the station. *Reptile saliva, how could that be?* She thought remembering the slime covered body of Sally Donaldson. Instead of going directly to the station she changed her mind where the road forked and headed toward the compound. Carolyn parked her jeep near the pond, she just wanted a quick look around. She made her way to the edge of the water noticing how thick the cattails had become all around the edge except for here where the pond abutted the compound land. Even though the sun was hot on her shoulders she shivered at the malevolent aura of the place. *Stop being silly, I must be really tired.* Carolyn mentally shook herself but she unsnapped the strap which held her revolver in its holster. The sun sparkled brilliantly on the water and it was hard seeing into its murky depths. She crouched down, shading her eyes, straining to get a better angle because the sun's reflections on water momentarily blinded her. It was already too late when she heard the violent rustle of the nearby cattails.

It lay among the tall cattails, unmoving. The sun luxuriously warmed its muscular body. The wounds of the night before had already started to heal. It felt lethargic in the humid heat of the day. A car stopped on the road near the swamp, a woman got out and walked toward the pond. It became instantly alert. It knew this prey, it had come close to attacking her once before.

It watched as the woman crouched by the pond. Its eyes widened slightly, intent on its prey. Its tongue flicked in and out rapidly. It began to inch forward, the heavy muscles of the long body propelling it without a sound through the cattails and undergrowth.

Sam had slept fitfully. Suddenly he woke with a start. He'd been dreaming of Carolyn and in the dream she was being menaced by something beyond his vision. Pulling himself fully awake, he couldn't decipher what woke him. He quickly took a cold shower trying to get the sleep cobwebs out of his mind. The feeling of dread persisted. He wondered if he should call Carolyn, if she was awake yet or would she still be out cold. Sam compromised; he called the station.

Officer Bell recognized Sam from the incidents of the night before. "I'm sorry sir, but Detective White hasn't come in yet. She said she'd be here over a half hour ago, when we called her about the state lab report. It's not like her to be late and not report in.

"State lab report?"

The officer hesitated not knowing if he should release this information. However, seeing as how Sam was so involved in the case he took the chance of getting in trouble and told Sam of the report. Sam suddenly knew where Carolyn was. Chills ran down his spine. He told the officer his suspicions and asked that a squad be sent. He was much closer and could be at the swamp in a couple moments.

Carolyn slowly became aware of the stillness surrounding her. All the creatures of the swamp and nearby woods had become completely silent. The air was sticky and breathless, not even a dragonfly moved. She stood. At the dry rustle behind her, she whirled around. She never got her gun out of its holster. It struck, snapping powerful jaws on Carolyn's arm, twisting and writhing to bring her to her knees. She was quickly engulfed, arms pinned unable to reach her gun. Her scream was cut off mid breath.

Sam saw Carolyn stand as he skidded up in his truck. Horrified he watched the big body hurl itself at Carolyn, bring her to the ground and encase her in its massive coils. Sam leaped out of the truck, grabbed his rifle, but even before he reached the whirling mass he knew he couldn't shoot, he'd hit Carolyn.

The writhing stopped and a horrible stillness ensued. Carolyn wasn't moving. The muscular coils began to contract with each breath Carolyn took. It squeezed tighter and tighter. Some instinct made Sam grab the snake's thick neck and squeeze. Hours later he wouldn't be able to explain why he did that or where he got the almost super-human strength to strangle the mighty creature.

When the first squad car arrived a few minutes later, Sam knew the monstrous reptile was dying.

"What the hell is that?" said one officer racing up to Sam. "Get a rescue squad out here," he shouted over his shoulder to his partner. He drew his gun.

"No, no," yelled Sam, "you'll hit her! Get it off her!!"

Sam never relaxed his grip until the snake was moved away from Carolyn's still body. He thought she was dead. There was blood everywhere from the gaping wound on her arm. He held his breath as he search for a pulse and finally found a soft flutter. Her chest was hardly moving and he was afraid to touch her. He did the only thing he could think to of, he blew air into her lungs hoping she could expel it on her own. He certainly couldn't push on her chest her ribs might be crushed.

It seemed to Sam it took the ambulance hours to arrive, but it was only moments. They had been returning from another call nearby and arrived soon after the officer radioed for them. The paramedics carefully moved Carolyn to a stretcher after putting an oxygen mask on her. Sam fussed at them until one of the medics had to tell him to get out of the way and let them do their job.

Just as Chief Daniels arrived they were loading a still unconscious Carolyn into the ambulance.

"What the hell's going on here," demanded the Chief to Sam, "I've been getting calls about giant snakes crushing Detective White."

"Over there," Sam pointed to the dead snake. "I'll tell you later, right now I'm following this ambulance." Sam matched actions to words and jumped into his truck and tore off.

The large snake was loaded into the back of a pick-up truck and taken to the local veterinarian. Several hours later the veterinarian would call the chief with a report of the contents of its stomach: Jeremy's medic alert bracelet and a pair of hoop earrings.

Chief Daniels stood for a few moments taking in the scene after the truck carrying the snake drove off. The shadow of a large bird flicked over him as it landed on a dead branch at the top of a nearby old oak. He raised his hand to shield his eyes and spoke to an officer walking toward him.

"That sure ain't no garter snake that eagle's got."

The great bird had a beautifully marked, thick-bodied young reptile in its beak, which kept trying to coil itself around the bird's head. The eagle shook the snake and lost its grip. The young snake smacked the pond's surface and quickly hid itself in the murky waters among the tall cattails where it had been born just days before.

K. Bastet is a Wisconsin writer who explores the subconscious fears we all have. Those things we tend to push to the back of our minds until they come slithering forth to invade our dreams.

K. Comstock is an artist skilled in various mediums, however pen and ink is her favorite. She resides by the shores of Lake Michigan in Kenosha, Wisconsin.

Made in the USA
Charleston, SC
07 March 2013